REAL LIFE

STORIES ABOUT
SURVIVING GANGS
AND BULLYING

Michaela Miller

W

FRANKLIN WATTS
LONDON·SYDNEY

First published in 2010 by Franklin Watts

Copyright © 2010 Arcturus Publishing Limited

Franklin Watts
338 Euston Road
London NW1 3BH

Franklin Watts Australia
Level 17/207 Kent Street, Sydney, NSW 2000

Produced by Arcturus Publishing Limited,
26/27 Bickels Yard, 151–153 Bermondsey Street, London SE1 3HA

Series concept: Alex Woolf
Editor and picture research: Alex Woolf
Designer: Ian Winton

Picture Credits:
Corbis: cover (Richard Hutchings), 6 (Image Source), 11 (Ausloeser), 12-13 (Image Source), 14-15 (Image Source), 16 (Anna Peisl), 17 (Anna Peisl), 20-21 (Image Source), 22 (Picture India), 23 (Timothy Tadder), 30 (Catherine Karnow), 31 (Paul A Souders), 34 (Steve Starr), 36 (Comstock), 38-39 (Image Source), 40 (Trevor Snapp), 41 (Oliver Rossi), 42 (Pawel Libera).
Getty Images: 7 (Yellow Dog Productions), 18-19 (Ulrik Tofte), 27 (Joos Mind), 32-33 (Doug Menuez), 35 (SW Productions), 37 (Robin Beck/AFP), 43 (Jon Bradley).
Shutterstock: 8-9 (Tad Denson), 10 (dragon_fang), 24-25 (Monkey Business Images), 28-29 (Justin Paget).

A CIP catalogue record for this book is available from the British Library.

Dewey Decimal Classification Number: 302.3

ISBN 978 1 4451 0072 2

Printed in China

Franklin Watts is a division of Hachette Children's Books, an Hachette UK company.
www.hachette.co.uk

SL001049EN

Contents

Introduction 1: Bullying

Being bullied can change someone's life forever, destroying confidence and stopping them from doing the things they enjoy. In extreme cases bullying can even lead to suicide. But it doesn't have to be this way. Young people all over the world have survived the terrible distress that bullying has caused them by getting the help and support they need. Their stories are all very different and in some cases truly shocking, but all show that bullies can be beaten.

What is bullying?

Bullying involves a person or a group deliberately using their power to make another person or a group feel bad on a regular basis. Bullying can happen to almost anyone. It can include teasing, calling someone names, threatening or harassing them. It can also be physical: bullies may attack their victims – hitting them, spitting at them, tripping them up, pushing them downstairs, or taking or damaging their belongings. Ignoring someone, excluding them from friendship groups or making sure they don't have partners for group work in school are also forms of bullying.

Bullying isn't only something that happens between children. Adults – including parents and teachers – can bully children and children can bully adults. There have been cases of children bullying adults who suffer from disabilities and of children bullying their teachers and parents. Adults can also bully each other at work.

◄ The American website www.Stop-Bullies.com reports that a girl is bullied every seven minutes in the playground, stairwell, classroom or toilets and that 85 per cent of the time, no one in authority stops it.

▶ Bullies often persuade others to work with them and use tactics that range from verbal abuse to physical violence. One US survey of 15,000 schoolchildren revealed that 23 per cent of boys and 11 per cent of girls reported bullying others in school either sometimes or weekly.

Why bully?

Bullying is a complicated issue and there are a lot of reasons why some people do it. They may see it as a way of being popular or of making themselves look tough and in charge in front of the people they want to impress. Some do it because they are jealous of the person they are bullying. Others sometimes do it because they are being bullied themselves. Because they are made to feel powerless by bullying directed at them, being horrible to someone else gives them some power back and they start to feel better.

Bullying statistics

- 69 per cent of children in the UK report being bullied.

- 58 per cent of children in the United States admit that someone has said mean or hurtful things to them online.

- Each year at least 20 children in the UK commit suicide because they are being bullied.

- In Australia 20 per cent of bullied children frequently stay away from school.

- In Canada a child is bullied every seven minutes in the playground and every 25 minutes in the classroom.

Who are the targets?

Some young people are bullied for no particular reason, but sometimes people are bullied because they are different in some way. It could be the colour of their skin, the country they come from, the way they talk, the way they dress, the things they like to do, their size or their name. It can also be because they don't have many friends or won't stand up for themselves.

Introduction 2: Gangs

Many young people join gangs willingly without realizing that the effects of membership on their lives can be devastating. Others are bullied into it. At first gangs can seem to give a sense of family, excitement, respect and protection. But they can lead to a life of crime, poverty and fear. Fortunately some young people around the world, no matter how difficult their circumstances, are now making the brave decision to say no to gangs.

About gangs

A gang can sound like quite a friendly thing – just a group of people with similar interests and goals that create a sense of belonging and security. But gangs can also mean groups that intimidate people, behave violently and get involved in crime. Gangs may have a territory, or 'turf', around their neighbourhood and will fight 'wars' with other gangs or people who they don't want on their patch. Every day young people are killed or injured as a result of gang conflict.

The bigger the gang the more people it has to fight for territory or to make money through crime. Gangs are therefore often on the lookout for new members. Some gangs put a lot of pressure on young people in their neighbourhood to join and increase their numbers. Gangs usually have symbols – certain clothes, colours, jewellery, tattoos or graffiti signs – unique to them and their members. Many have their own language – hand signs and words – and their own music.

Joining a gang

Young people join gangs for many reasons. They may be seeking protection from bullies, or a chance to make money, or the feeling of family that they don't have at home. They may be continuing a tradition – their families may be members. Or they may simply want the thrill of being linked with something that seems tough and exciting.

Some gangs have violent initiation ceremonies such as 'beating' or 'jumping' in. This can involve someone who wants to be a member being beaten up by gang members and not showing fear. In other cases, people may be asked to commit crimes such as muggings or drive-by shootings in order to become members.

Leaving the gang

It is not always easy to leave a gang. The remaining gang members may fear that those who leave will tell the police about their activities. Gang members have been killed for trying to leave or for becoming police informers. Some gangs allow members to be

American gang facts

- 14 per cent of teens are gang members.

- 89 per cent of serious violent crimes committed by teens are committed by gang members.

- Gang members are 60 per cent more likely to be killed than non gang members.

- The average age of a gang member is 17–18 years old.

- Police reports indicate that 6 per cent of gang members are female and that 39 per cent of gangs have female members.

'jumped' out, or beaten up, to receive the gang's permission to exit. Others leave by gradually spending less time with the gang, by finding new friends and new interests.

This book tells the stories of some young victims of gangs and bullying, the difficulties they encountered and how they survived. The stories are all true, but names and in some cases locations have been changed to protect the people involved.

▲ Gangs can influence young people's lives at school. Some gangs see schools as recruitment centres where they can find new members and will even try to claim schools as gang territory.

Brea and Braiden's Story
Canada

Brea Lawrenson and Braiden Turner had similar experiences of being bullied – their schoolmates teased them about their weight. Both developed eating disorders as a result and felt terribly alone. Fortunately they found each other, shared their stories and are now using their musical talents to spread their anti-bullying message throughout Canada.

When she was seven, Braiden changed school. She soon became a victim of relentless bullying that lasted until she was 17. The bullies didn't like her because she looked different – she was taller than everyone else in her new school and slightly overweight. She was also very good at singing and music, and the bullies didn't like that either.

Eventually, their cruelty damaged Braiden's health. When a boy made jokes about her weight in front of the whole class, she was humiliated and decided to take drastic action. She dieted, eventually losing so much weight that she developed an eating disorder. Still the bullying continued. Looking back, Braiden remembers only one girl who stood up for her and anyone else who was being bullied, but even she couldn't help Braiden feel better about herself.

Finally, Braiden was approached by one of her teachers. He told her he was very worried about her health. He talked about eating disorders and how they can end in death. He looked so concerned and upset that Braiden realized she had a serious problem. With her parents she decided to get counselling and medical help for her eating disorder. She also threw herself into her music.

While practising at her music studio she met Brea Lawrenson, who was also a musician and two years older. Braiden discovered that Brea was also recovering from an eating disorder that had developed because of bullying about her weight. The girls became close friends. They wrote songs about their experiences that they hoped would encourage people to think about bullying and stamp it out.

What sort of people bully?

Bullies come in all shapes and sizes. Some are bigger or taller than everyone. Some get into trouble a lot. Some are popular and get good grades at school. But most bullies have one thing in common — they usually bully to make themselves feel better. And if someone has grown up with bullying behaviour at home — for example, being hit or told how stupid they are, they may feel this behaviour is normal. They may not even understand how wrong their behaviour is.

▶ Brea and Braiden have used their shared love of music and performing to speak out against bullying. Their song 'Black and Purple' (see page 12) is a theme song for the Canadian Red Cross's anti-bullying campaign.

When they both left high school, they asked the organizers of an anti-bullying campaign in Canada if they could help. Now, as anti-bullying campaigners, Brea and Braiden tour schools around the country, using their music and stories to encourage people who are being bullied to tell someone – a teacher, parent or anyone who can help.

They also talk about bystanders – people who may not bully, but see it happen. Bystanders can play a powerful role in stamping out bullying, either by standing up for victims of bullying or by reporting the bullying to an adult who can help. Canadian research has shown that in 50 per cent of cases, bystanders can stop the bullying in less than 10 seconds by speaking out.

Peter's Story
Australia

As a bully, 14-year-old Peter felt like he was 'king' of his school. He was big for his age and believed that by picking on students who seemed weak and small he was able to make himself appear even bigger and more important. The school was very unhappy with his behaviour, and he had few real friends, but he refused to change until one day he read an inspiring book.

The book contained a powerful image. It showed a taunted white bear slamming his 15-year-old tormentor to the ground, leaving the boy broken, alone and helpless for several days. Seeing that image helped Peter change his life. Peter found the book – *Touching Spirit Bear* by Ben Mikaelsen – while he was in day-long isolation for bullying.

His teacher, disgusted with Peter's behaviour, had requested isolation to punish him and to give other pupils some space. Peter's victims that week had been two girls he had repeatedly bullied for being small. He also told them they were ugly, fat, covered in spots and anything else he could think of to make them feel miserable. He laughed at their distress and, when confronted by teachers about it, he refused to apologize.

Angry and bored in the isolation room, Peter picked up the most violent-looking book he could find. The cover showed a huge white bear towering over a boy armed with a knife. He imagined himself killing the bear, thought it was just his type of book and started to read. But what he found in its pages shocked him.

It was the story of a bullying and violent boy who had beaten up another boy so badly that he suffered brain damage and had to be hospitalized. Like Peter, the boy was put in isolation, but on a remote Alaskan island. Still thinking he was invincible and that he could do what he liked, the boy decided to kill the white bear he had seen on the island. The boy's attitude, the terrible injuries he suffered from the bear and his attempts to turn himself into a better person with the help of his Native American parole officer, captivated Peter.

Black and Purple

He has to stand up and be strong
To show everyone he belongs
She has to fight to live her life
She has to hide her pain inside

And everyone is scared of him
But that's the way that he's gotta live
Do you think she feels his pain
There's no justice in this game

And when they fall asleep at night
They know the morning won't be bright
'Cause they are living in a hell
Yeah they're trapped inside themselves

Brea Lawrenson and Braiden Turner
Theme song to Canadian Red Cross anti-bullying campaign

▲ **Bullies usually feel they need to control others and to make themselves seem more powerful. They often target people who are quiet, easily pushed around and have few friends. Underneath their tough exteriors, bullies may be angry or depressed because of personal troubles at home or at school.**

The book showed him that he was bully. Like the boy in the story, he had anger management problems. With help from his teachers and parents, Peter started to change his behaviour. He apologized to his victims, both at school and in front of their parents. He has worked on the anti-bullying policy of his school and now does his best to look out for and help those who seem weaker than himself. He also now finds that he has real friends rather than people who just hang around with him because they're scared not to.

Sean's Story
United Kingdom

Sean is mixed race and grew up in an area where there were few other mixed-race children or people of different cultures. At primary and secondary school he was bullied because of his colour. When Sean decided to take action, he changed his school for the better.

Sean remembers first being bullied at primary school when he was around six or seven years old. A classmate made remarks about his colour and where he came from. This was Sean's first encounter with racism. He told his parents who complained to the school, but the bully continued with his racist comments when he thought he could get away with them. Sean got on with his work, kept to his circle of friends and tried his best to ignore the boy.

What is racism?

The world's population can be divided into groups on the basis of physical characteristics such as skin and hair colour or eye shape. These groups are called races. Racism is a belief that people of different races have different qualities and abilities and that some races are superior to others. Racists sometimes bully people of other races. They may do this by name-calling or violence. They also try to get other people on their side by trying to convince them that their racist beliefs are right. Some political parties have racist beliefs. They say that people of different races should not live in their country.

Sean hoped the problem would disappear when he went to secondary school, but it got worse. This time Sean was not only made to feel bad because of his colour – people also ganged up on him because of his intelligence and because he was good at drama. A classmate started calling him a 'geek'. Whenever he read aloud, answered questions in class or was praised by a teacher, there were snickers and comments from other students. Some people spread his mobile phone number around and he began receiving insulting text messages.

Sean lost friends because they were scared of the bullies and he felt very alone. Finally, when he was 15 and feeling very low, he found the courage to tell a teacher who he knew liked him. The teacher took the matter very seriously. Other teachers were notified about the problem and Sean started to get the support he needed.

The bullies were confronted and the whole school worked hard to combat racism. Sean was pleased to take a major role in the fight against bullying by speaking to other students and teachers. He highlighted the problems that racism and bullying cause. With his

▲ Schools have a duty to protect their students from racist behaviour. In Britain it is a legal requirement to have a race equality policy. All schools should also have an anti-bullying policy that teachers, students and the school's governing body agree to and understand.

teachers' support he started an anti-bullying campaign and became the school's anti-bullying coordinator. He helped to organize support groups for young people being bullied, encouraged the school to appoint anti-bullying ambassadors and even made anti-bullying films to raise awareness of the problem.

As an adult, Sean is a well-known anti-bullying campaigner who has won national awards for his work. He runs training sessions for students and teachers to help prevent bullying. He also runs anti-bullying events and activities that have been attended by thousands of people.

15

Noelle's Story
Australia

When Noelle was 13 years old, she felt like she was falling in love with her best friend. Confused and wanting to be honest she decided to talk about her feelings. Sadly, this decision led to Noelle being bullied, but her courage and the need to be true to herself helped her survive.

Noelle and Sara met when they were 11 in the first year at their all-girls school. They became great friends, sharing the same sense of humour, each others' clothes and love of music. But when Noelle was 13, she began to feel differently about Sara. She felt her stomach jolt when she looked at her and wanted to be with her all the time. She started to feel like she was falling in love with her best friend.

Noelle kept her feelings to herself for several weeks, but during a school holiday she found she was thinking of Sara more and more. Eventually she decided to tell Sara how she felt. It wasn't easy, and Noelle cried as she told her. Sara was horrified, walked away and immediately told a group of their mutual friends. Noelle was excluded from the group. Sara refused to look at Noelle or speak to her and soon the whole school knew about Noelle's confession.

▶ Although good friends hope they will care about each other for ever, this is not always the case. An incident or misunderstanding can sometimes cause friends to break up, and one or both may feel that they never want to their relationship to be the same again. Such break-ups can also lead to bullying.

What is homophobia?

Homophobia is a hatred, resentment or fear of homosexuals. Homosexuals are people who feel a romantic or sexual attraction towards people who are the same sex as them. Some homophobic people keep their feelings to themselves; others may be verbally aggressive or even behave violently towards homosexual people.

Noelle tried to make it up to Sara, to tell her that she was still the same person. She said that it didn't mean anything and that she would never try to kiss her or express her affection in any way, but Sara wouldn't listen. Noelle found herself alone and friendless. She didn't tell her parents or her teachers about her unhappiness because she felt ashamed. During the summer holiday she hung around with the people in her neigbourhood who she had been to primary school with, and she started to feel better.

▲ When Noelle confessed her feelings about Sara, she was bullied. The girls deliberately ignored her and excluded her from things. Although these tactics do not seem as obvious as physical violence, they cause great hurt and distress and should always be seen as bullying behaviour.

But when summer ended and Noelle went back to school, Sara and her other former friends still wanted nothing to do with her. Then, gradually, Noelle realized that not everybody at school despised her. Some people didn't mind when she sat beside them in class or at lunch. Slowly she started to make new friends and trust people again.

Noelle is now 16 and still not sure of her sexuality, because she is attracted to boys as well. She thinks her feelings for Sara may have been a phase she was going through or it may mean that she is bisexual. She feels her experience has made her stronger and has no regrets about telling Sara how she felt. She also always makes a point of speaking out against homophobia and bullying.

Heinz's Story
Germany

Heinz has always been deaf in one ear. This makes it quite difficult to work out which direction sound is coming from, so Heinz has to be very careful when crossing roads. He also finds it hard to understand what other people are saying when there is background noise. Heinz was badly bullied at school because of his disability. He had few friends because he seemed different. But volunteering changed his life.

When Heinz went to primary school, he was given a hearing aid. His teacher and parents made sure that everyone in the class knew of his hearing difficulty. Heinz had no problems with bullying at that time. But when he went to secondary school, it all changed.

Disability and bullying

Research shows that young people with disabilities are twice as likely to be bullied as anyone else. They are usually targeted simply because they are different. Disabilities can include physical problems such as deafness, visual impairment, speech and coordination difficulties, deformities of the body, and illnesses such as asthma and epilepsy. Children with learning difficulties, special educational needs and behaviour problems are targeted, too — often because the bullies find them irritating and easy to pick on. Some children with learning difficulties find it harder to communicate than other people of their age and they are taunted by bullies as a result.

A group of boys started to pick on him – they made fun of his hearing aid. They called him stupid and pretended to talk to him when they weren't. They opened and shut their mouths as if they were talking, but no sound would come out. Other children thought this was very funny. When teachers they saw this, they would tell the students to stop. But the teachers couldn't be with Heinz every minute of day, and he felt very alone with his problems.

Then physical attacks started. He was stabbed with pens, kicked and punched. Although his parents complained and the bullies were punished, they still continued to be unkind when the teachers were not looking. No students stood up for him. Heinz eventually found it easier to spend his breaks and lunchtimes alone in the school library, hiding from the bullies. He eventually left school to be home educated.

▲ Research has shown that bullying can have a negative effect on children's mental health. Children who are bullied are more likely to have lower self-esteem and suffer from depression or other mental health problems. Victims of bullying are also often absent from or dislike school.

By the time he was 17, Heinz had lost so much confidence that he couldn't bring himself to go out and make new friends. Then the family doctor made a suggestion. He encouraged Heinz to join a local volunteer network that helped with gardening projects around his city. On his first day Heinz was amazed at the friendliness of everyone and the fun they all had. He enjoyed being out in the fresh air and doing something useful. He met a couple of other volunteers who had been bullied too. They all shared their experiences and made each other feel better.

Heinz is now a regular volunteer. His work in the city gardens gave him the confidence to study horticulture at college. His days of being bullied are over.

Rachel's Story
New Zealand

Rachel thought that working hard at school and being helpful was what you were supposed to do. Sadly, some of her classmates thought differently. She became the victim of vicious verbal and physical attacks. But a caring head teacher changed her life.

Rachel remembers that going to school was, at first, a very happy time. Putting her hand up, giving the right answers and getting praise made her feel really good. But soon she was being teased by some girls for all the praise she was getting.

One girl, Jane, was the ringleader. She made sure Rachel was either left out of their make-believe games or included only in ones where she had to be the character no one else wanted to be – such as the dog or slave that had to be ordered about. No matter how hard Rachel tried to make the girls like her, nothing changed. She told her mother, but her mother's response was: 'What are you are doing to make them treat you like this?'

At secondary school the physical bullying started. Jane and her ever-growing group of friends kicked and hit the back of Rachel's chair, spat and threw food at her, ripped up her homework and stole

▶ These girls are bullying their victim emotionally by whispering in front of her to make her feel left out. Other types of emotional bullying can include name-calling, rumour-spreading, and being friends one week and then turning against the victim the next for no reason.

Emotional and physical abuse

Emotional abuse is making another person feel bad by humiliating them or hurting their feelings. For example, telling someone they are ugly, fat, stupid or worthless is emotional abuse. It's wrong, even if it is said jokingly. Physical abuse is deliberately hurting or injuring another person. It can include hitting, kicking, beating with objects, throwing and shaking. Physical abuse can cause pain, cuts, bruising, broken bones and sometimes even death.

her things. One day Rachel's gym kit disappeared. She later found bits of it strewn all around the school playing field. Some teachers tried to deal with the problem. One noticed Jane throwing food at Rachel and gave Jane a detention, but Jane's behaviour became even worse. One gym class, after being tripped up and pushed around, Rachel snapped and hit Jane back. Rachel was given detention.

In desperation she went to the head teacher and told her everything. The head teacher was very sympathetic and talked to other teachers and students. The bullies were called in and given a talking to, and the situation got better for a while. Then, one day, Rachel was cornered in a classroom by Jane and her friends. They held her arm against a hot radiator until it burned, before running off. Rachel went to the school nurse and said it happened by accident. The nurse and head teacher didn't believe her and persuaded Rachel to tell them the full story. Jane's parents were called and she was suspended from the school for two weeks.

One term later, Jane pushed Rachel down the stairs in front of witnesses and was expelled by the head teacher. For her last two years of school Rachel was left in peace. She had little confidence and only one or two friends, but worked hard to put the bullying behind her. Rachel is training to be a teacher herself and wants to be just like the head teacher who took a firm stand against bullying.

Anoop's Story
India

Anoop was sent to boarding school by his mother because she wanted him to receive a good education. As a single parent she also hoped that he would meet male teachers whom he could learn from and look up to. Sadly, Anoop was badly bullied, both by other boys and by a teacher.

When Anoop was a baby, his father died in a plane crash. Anoop and his mother moved in with his grandparents. When he was seven, his grandparents decided he should go to boarding school, just as his father had done at that age.

Anoop was devastated by the news. He cried himself to sleep for weeks before leaving home. His mother cried, too, but was convinced by her parents-in-law that it was the right thing to do. They said Anoop needed strong, educated, male role models, and the best place to find them was at his father's old school.

When Anoop arrived, he thought it wasn't too bad. He slept in a dormitory, and although he was homesick, he liked the companionship of the other boys. He also liked his class teacher, who was strict but friendly.

But then the teacher left, and Mr Shah arrived. Mr Shah was sporty, young and handsome. The boys wanted to do well to please him. But Anoop could never do as well as Mr Shah expected.

◀ Most people become teachers because they are enthusiastic about their subject, they want to support their students and help them do their best. A friendly and trusted teacher is someone who should be able to help you if you have a problem with bullying.

▶ Bullying by a teacher is unacceptable and must not be tolerated. If you feel that you are being treated badly by a teacher, speak to a trusted adult about it.

He made sure the whole class was aware of Anoop's shortcomings. He told them Anoop was lazy and made fun of his poor writing and reading. Everyone thought it was hilarious. Soon Anoop began to feel frightened and sick at the thought of being taught by Mr Shah – he felt tired, run down and completely miserable.

When he returned home for the holidays, Anoop's mother noticed he wasn't himself and had started sleepwalking. She asked what was wrong and he told her the whole story. She complained to the school's principal, who talked to Mr Shah. He did not take the complaint well. The bullying grew worse and Mr Shah seemed to be encouraging other students to pick on Anoop, too.

Eventually Anoop's mother decided to move him to a different school. Anoop waited anxiously for the bullying to begin again at the new school. But it didn't. He made lots of friends and the teachers were kind and enthusiastic. They discovered Anoop had dyslexia, which is why he had found spelling and reading so hard.

What can you do if a teacher is a bully?

It is part of a teacher's job to look after children and treat them fairly. Teachers should never make their students feel stupid, call them names or give them unfair punishments. If you are being bullied by a teacher at your school, talk to another member of staff whom you trust and tell them what is happening. It's also important to tell your parents or guardians about the problem. You should keep a record of any incidents of bullying, including times and dates, to back up your case.

Anoop never forgot how powerless and vulnerable Mr Shah made him feel. When he finished university, he made up his mind to get a job helping children in distress. He now works for an organization that helps children who live in poverty and suffering all over the world.

Laurence's Story
Portugal

Seventeen-year-old Laurence was good at sports and popular with both boys and girls in his class. He had never had a problem with bullying, until one day he noticed people were looking at him differently.

Laurence had always been happy at school. He had a small group of friends and was a respected football player, but the year he injured his knee was not good. The operation to repair the injury took a long time to get over. He also felt very hurt when his girlfriend broke up with him. He first realized that something was not right when he noticed people he didn't know looking at him in the school corridors, giggling and then looking away. Then people starting saying strange things to him, such as: 'How's Senhor Silva?'

Senhor Silva was Laurence's football coach and biology teacher. He had been really supportive about Laurence's knee injury. He told him to be patient and not to worry – he'd be back playing football soon enough. Laurence didn't understand why people would want to tease him about Senhor Silva.

He asked his friends what was going on, but they said they didn't understand it either. Then one of them saw a blog site on the Internet, set up in Laurence's name. The fake blog had been created by some girls in the year below. The girls had taken pictures from one of Laurence's genuine social networking sites and altered them to make it look as though Laurence was having an homosexual relationship with Senhor Silva. The entries in the blog gave the impression that Laurence had lost his girlfriend because of this. There were comments from other people at school, too, and it seemed like everyone was in on it.

Laurence was very distressed – he felt abused and humiliated. However, he knew what he had to do. He went straight to Senhor Silva and told him what had happened. Senhor Silva

Protect yourself online

- Don't reply to any unpleasant messages, as this may encourage the bullies.

- Keep a copy of any abusive emails or messages and make a note of when you received them.

- Never give out personal details on the Internet, such as your real name, address, age or phone number. Even telling someone which school you go to can help them find out information about you.

- If you receive unpleasant messages, change your online nicknames or user ID to something different, block the email addresses they came from and/or complain to the host website.

▶ Cyber-bullying can be carried out 24 hours a day, seven days a week, making the victim a continual target. A single message posted online can remain there indefinitely, damaging someone's social life and friendships.

reported it to the head teacher. The girls who were believed to be responsible were interviewed. They denied it, but the head teacher, who had conducted his own investigation, was not convinced. He asked for help from the local police, who tracked the girls' computer use.

The girls then admitted their crime. They said they had done it because Laurence thought he was too good for them and had been unkind to one of their friends who had wanted to go out with him. Laurence was amazed. He didn't even know them or the girl they were talking about. The girls were cautioned by the police and suspended from school for several weeks. Laurence worked hard to forget that the incident had ever happened.

Charlotte's Story
United Kingdom

Charlotte is a bright, lively girl. She is friendly and independent with a strong sense of fun. She couldn't believe it when she started at a new school and her outgoing nature made her a victim of cyber-bullying.

When Charlotte joined a large sixth-form college, she felt she was having the time of her life. She loved the social scene, the parties and meeting new people. At one party she talked for a long time with a boy from her drama class who she hadn't really spoken to before. As she was leaving to go home with her friends, he asked for her phone number. Charlotte happily gave it to him.

The next day he asked if she wanted to meet for a coffee after drama. Charlotte agreed. As they were chatting in the canteen, she noticed a table of girls – a couple of whom she knew

Mobile phone privacy tips

If you receive text messages that make you feel uncomfortable, ask a parent or teacher for help. They can help you work with the mobile phone company to trace the identity of anyone sending unpleasant text messages.

- Don't reply to any nasty messages you receive.

- Keep the messages that you have been sent so they can be used as evidence.

- Don't answer any calls that are from a withheld number or from a number you don't know.

- Change your mobile number and only give out your new number to close friends.

- If the problem is serious, you and the adult you have told should report it to the police.

– looking at her and then quickly looking away. She walked by their table on her way out and smiled, but they didn't smile back. She was sure that as soon as her back was turned she heard someone swear at her.

That night, on MSN, Charlotte was shocked to find herself being talked about in a really nasty way. She was being accused of stealing Rob from Beth, a girl she vaguely knew. Charlotte defended herself, saying she had only just met him and he was just a friend. But the girls wouldn't listen and the abuse continued into the night. Then, as Charlotte was going to sleep, her phone beeped with a text message. She couldn't believe it: Beth had got her number and was telling her to keep away from Rob.

This was just the beginning. The MSN and text abuse continued over several weeks. Charlotte's mother told her to change her number and not to use MSN, but Charlotte wouldn't because she wanted to keep in touch with her friends. She did, however, let her personal tutor know what was happening. He told the head of the college and asked Charlotte to keep a record of all the abuse. When Beth threatened to 'get her', Charlotte took her records to her personal tutor. Beth was interviewed and asked to leave. The texts and MSN hate campaign stopped.

Two months later, Charlotte saw Beth in a nearby town. Beth ran over, pushed Charlotte to the ground and kicked her. Charlotte was badly shaken, but she went straight to the police and told them her story. Beth was interviewed and warned to have no further contact with Charlotte, otherwise there would be serious consequences. Charlotte has not heard from Beth since then.

◀ **Although it is distressing, cyber-bullying can be traced and stopped. Each time someone accesses the Internet, an IP (Internet Protocol) address – a type of electronic fingerprint – is established. This IP address can be used by the authorities to trace all electronic communications between computers and/or mobile phones.**

Alice's Story
United States

Alice's stepfather forced her to have sex with him when she was 13. She was devastated by the attack, but found the strength to make sure he was brought to justice.

Alice had never known her father – for many years she lived alone with her mother. One day, just after Alice's ninth birthday, her mother arrived home with a boyfriend – Ben. Ben was funny, entertaining and kind. Alice really liked him and was pleased when a year later her mother married him. For the first time she felt she had someone who could be a dad. Ben came to her school plays and concerts, cheered her on when she played softball, looked after her when her mother was at work and was happy to watch DVDs with her and listen to her school gossip.

But one night, when her mother was at work and Alice was 13, Ben came into her room and forced her to have sex with him. Alice was devastated by the attack – she felt hurt, betrayed and angry with herself. Ben had told her it was her fault and warned Alice not to tell her mother. He said that if she did, it would destroy the marriage and make her mother very unhappy. He then offered her money to keep quiet. But Alice knew that what he had done was wrong and she had to tell her mother. As soon as she and her mother were alone in the house, Alice told her what had happened. Her mother was deeply shocked, called the police and took Alice to hospital.

The police arrested Ben, but he was let out on bail with a restraining order, which meant he was not allowed to go anywhere near Alice or her mother. However, one day, Alice was horrified to find him following her as she walked to school. She reported it and he was put in jail until the trial.

Three years later, the case came to trial. Alice had to go to court and tell the jury everything that had happened. She also had to look at Ben in the courtroom, which made

What is sexual abuse?

Sexual abuse is when:

- you're being touched in a way you don't like

- you're being forced to have sex

- you're forced to look at sexual pictures or videos

- you're made to watch someone do something sexual, including exposing themselves to you

- you're made to do something sexual to someone, which feels uncomfortable or wrong

If you are being sexually abused, you must report it to someone you trust who can help you, such as a teacher, the police or a relative.

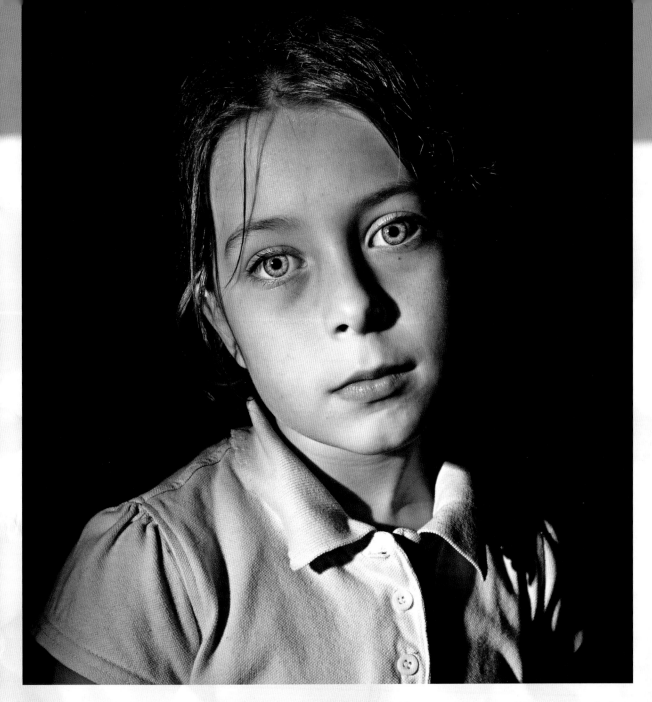

▲ There are lots of reasons why young people do not tell anyone about sexual abuse. These can include being threatened or bribed by their abuser to keep quiet; fear that no one will believe them; blaming themselves for the abuse; or feeling too ashamed or embarrassed to tell.

her feel shaky and sick. Ben's lawyer tried to get Alice to say that it hadn't really happened and tried to confuse her, but it didn't work. Despite her fear, she stuck to her story.

Ben was found guilty and sent to prison for ten years. Alice finished high school with the highest grades in her class. She says that she will never forget what happened, but she has learned to deal with it and has no regrets about reporting what Ben did and bringing him to justice.

SECTION 2: GANGS

Carlos's Story

Philippines

At Carlos's school in the Philippines it felt like just about everyone was in a gang or thinking of joining one. Although Carlos was frightened of what might happen if he didn't join, he decided to do something different for his impoverished community.

Carlos lived near the city dump. His dad was a tricycle taxi driver and his mother looked after Carlos and his brothers and sisters. The family had little money. His parents told him to work hard at school so that he could get a good education and make a better life for himself.

Carlos did his best to do this, but he lived in a community dominated by gangs. The gangs made money by committing crimes. They stole, they used and sold drugs and they fought with other gangs. Members of some gangs waited outside the school gates and there were

▲ A slum in Manila, the capital city of the Philippines. Half the people in the Philippines live on less than two US dollars (about £1.30) a day. Many survive by scavenging food and recyclables from tips and other people's rubbish bins. Around 3.5 million Filipino people live in slums.

Street children

As many as 100 million children live on their own on the streets of hundreds of cities around the world. They live a hand-to-mouth existence, struggling to survive from one day to the next. In some countries, street children are routinely detained, beaten, tortured and sometimes killed by the police. UNICEF estimates that nearly a million children enter the sex trade every year. Many of these will be street children.

▶ **A young boy from a Manila slum. In the Philippines, teenage membership of urban gangs has reached an estimated 130,000 in 2010.**

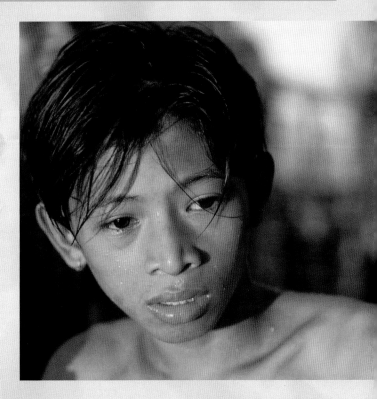

gangs in the school as well. They created a negative and intimidating atmosphere. Most of the children in Carlos's neighbourhood were members of a gang and they bullied him to try and join too. A few times he was beaten up because he wouldn't join, but he knew that in his city, gang membership usually led to prison and sometimes an early death.

When he was in the fourth year of secondary school, the bullying got worse, and gang members started to throw rocks at him. Carlos decided to join forces with three other young people he knew who were also trying to escape the gangs. They formed a friendship group and joined an organization trying to improve conditions in Carlos's city. The organization gave them support and asked them to help out with some of their improvement projects. Carlos also decided to train to be a teacher – he wanted to use education as a means of helping people out of poverty and away from the gangs.

Today, Carlos runs an organization of more than a hundred volunteers, who teach in the slums. They wheel carts through the streets, providing the young people who come to them with a free education. The carts are stocked with books, pens, tables and chairs. This enables the volunteers to create a school setting in unconventional locations such as cemeteries and rubbish dumps. The group also runs a hygiene clinic, where children can get a bath and learn how to brush their teeth.

Carlos's group has educated more than 1,500 children in the city's slums. He has received recognition from the Philippine government and an award for his achievements from an international television network.

Darielle's Story
United States

Darielle joined a gang when she was very young. For a long time she managed to keep it a secret from her parents, and gradually the gang took over her life. As people around her began to die from gang violence, she realized she had to make a change for the better.

Darielle is an only child who grew up in a neighbourhood known for being gang territory. Her father, of Mexican descent, was an alcoholic. His parents had been Pachuchos – Mexican gang members – in the 1950s. Darielle started hanging around with gang members when she was eight years old and liked the sense of belonging it gave her.

Things were not good at home because of her father's drink problem. She hid her gang contacts from her parents and said she was just out playing with friends from school.

When she was 11, Darielle was 'jumped' – initiated into the gang. For this she had to be hit for two minutes by four 16-year-old boys from the gang. She came home black and blue with bruises and told her mother she had got into a fight at school. Darielle's life spiralled into violence. She took part in drive-bys – driving along and shooting at cars, property and people linked with members of rival gangs. In her first year as a true gang member, five members of her gang were killed.

> **Girls in US gangs**
> - There are around 80,000 female gang members in the United States, of which approximately 32,000 are teenagers.
> - 10 per cent of US gang members are female.
> - 60 per cent of US gangs do not allow female members.
> - 2 per cent of US gangs are composed of girls only.

During Darielle's first seven years as a gang member, 46 people from her neighbourhood died through gang violence, but still she stayed in the gang and took part in the drive-bys. One night the man she was driving with was shot by a rival gang at a traffic light. Shocked, she sat in the car spattered with his blood until she was taken to hospital.

Even this was not enough to persuade Darielle to leave. When she was 20 she was arrested for a gang murder – a murder she didn't commit. The police realized they had made a mistake and Darielle was released without charge. Afterwards she told some of the senior members that she wanted out. She knew that leaving the gang could involve being 'jumped' out – beaten up. But she was told she had their respect and could go.

Darielle went home and has never looked back. She still lives in the neighbourhood, still speaks to the gang members who were her friends, but never takes part in violence. Her father died a year after she left the gang. She remains close to her mother.

◀ **Girls usually join gangs for the same reasons as boys. They often come from poor neighbourhoods and feel they have no family love or sense of belonging. The gang 'family' promises to give them all the things they want or need.**

Gina's Story
United States

When Gina, a young single mother, saw that her 13-year-old son Aaron was hanging around with members of Crips gang, she knew she had to take action. What she did changed Aaron's life for the better.

Gina's family had lived in the same deprived inner-city neighbourhood in Los Angeles for generations. Because of its high unemployment and rising crime rate, many older people, including Gina's mother, father and sister, had moved away. Gina, however, couldn't afford to move. Her husband had been shot in a hold-up at a nearby corner store when Aaron was ten. Now she and Aaron had to survive on what Gina earned as a waitress.

She was close to Aaron, but when he moved to secondary school, he changed. He no longer invited friends home, didn't tell Gina where he was going and stopped working hard at school. When Gina saw him hanging around with a group of older boys, she suspected he was being groomed for gang membership.

She spoke to a local community police officer about her concerns. He advised her to search Aaron's property for evidence of gang membership. Sure enough, in his school backpack, she found a blue scarf – the 'flag' of a large and violent Los Angeles gang, known as the Crips.

She confronted Aaron with this evidence. He admitted that to earn his place in the gang he had been sent on late night

▶ Crips gang members in Los Angeles. Being a member of a gang often involves owning and using guns. US research has shown that gang members are at least 60 times more likely to be killed than the rest of the population. This can be even higher in some cities.

◀ It is not always easy for parents to convince their children to leave gangs. This is because young people may feel that being a member of a gang is like belonging to a better and more important family.

missions into the territory of a rival gang, the Bloods, to mark their patch with Crips' graffiti. He had also been delivering drugs for dealers in the gang. He admitted he was scared of the violence and too frightened to leave the gang. Gina was terrified he would be hurt or killed if he remained involved with the Crips. They both agreed he had to get out.

Secretly, she arranged for him to move in with her sister, a seven-hour drive away. Gina and Aaron left for her sister's at 4 am one morning. A day later Gina returned to the city. She told the police officer what she had done and said she was frightened that the gang members would come in search of Aaron and threaten her. The police officer helped her install a CCTV system outside her home and arranged for undercover officers to regularly drive by her house to check that everything was OK.

A year later, Aaron is doing well at his new school. He has had counselling to help him put his old life behind him. Gina misses Aaron terribly, but says she has no regrets as she believes moving away has saved his life. Aaron tells her he never wants to come back to the old neighbourhood.

About relocation

Although relocation — leaving one area for another — can seem like a good solution to leaving gangs, it doesn't always work. Gang members have been known to track down those who have relocated, and in a few cases they have killed them. Relocations are usually done in secret so there are no statistics to say how successful these moves are. Some schools have found that young gang members who relocate to avoid a gang find it hard to stay away from gangs in their new neighbourhood. However, support and counselling can often help them to steer their life in a more positive direction.

Jay's Story
United States

Most families want to keep their children out of trouble, but not all members of Jay's family felt this way. His cousins forced him to join their neighbourhood gang.

When Jay was 12 his cousins didn't give him a cake and presents, they initiated him into their gang. Because Jay looked up to them, and they were family, it seemed quite natural. As a gang member, Jay felt like one of the cool kids and very powerful. His cousins gave him a gun and introduced him to drugs. Jay did whatever he was told and quickly climbed the ranks of the gang. One of his main jobs was to buy and sell drugs. He found being a gangster addictive. He enjoyed the language, the clothing, the tattoos, the music and the money.

Jay's cousins kept telling him it was okay to break the law. However, the rest of his family were law-abiding. His parents and younger brothers and sisters were upset by Jay's gang membership. But by this time the gang had become more important to him than anything – even his own family. Eventually Jay and his father stopped communicating – they didn't speak for three years.

Then, one night, everything changed. One of the gang's new recruits confided to Jay that he wanted to leave the gang. Jay told him it was impossible, but the young man invited

◀ Certain styles, types and colours of clothing, jewellery and shoes are associated with particular gangs, but some young people just wear gang style because they want to look cool. People with no connections to gangs have sometimes been attacked because they were wearing gang colours or style.

▶ A former gang member has his tattoo removed. Many gangs use tattoos to identify their members. Getting the tattoos removed once you have left the gang is a way to put your old life behind you. Gang tattoos can work against former members because employers associate them with crime and violence.

him to a meeting. It was a meeting of a support group run by ex-gang members who were helping young people wanting to leave gangs.

After that first meeting, Jay felt as though a light bulb had switched on in his head. He knew he had to get out. At first it seemed impossible – the gang had become everything to him. However, he started spending less time with the other members. He left town to live with a relative for a while to try and break ties with his old life. The other members didn't like it and some, including his cousins, threatened to kill him if he left. They thought he would tell their secrets and the crimes they had committed to the police. Jay ignored the threats.

It took him nearly a year, but Jay finally managed to escape from the gang. He is now living back at home. He meets with the support group every week and believes it has saved his life. With the help of the group Jay is also having his tattoos removed. Tattoos are an important part of gang membership. Members usually earn them by completing missions and proving their toughness.

Today, Jay is a completely different person. He is back at school and enjoys studying, particularly maths. He describes himself as having been through a lifetime already, but he feels safer now, with a future to look forward to.

started in violence,
turmoil to silence,
let's memorize names,
lost screams in the sirens,
kings an tyrants,
falling the same,
will you remember me for me,
or just my name,
i was given on the street,
i would creep,
til i sleep,
an rest in peace…

Part of a poem called 'Losses' by Jey Klug

Michael's Story
South Africa

At 16, Michael was a hardened gang member, running drugs, stealing and fighting in a South African township. But one night he walked away from his gang and since then he has been helping others walk away, too.

It was a typical Friday night. Michael set out to meet his gang with his knife thrust deep in his pocket. The gang was set to fight a rival gang and he knew that some of them, including him, could die. He had been fighting with the gang since he was 12 and couldn't imagine any other kind of life.

As he walked through the neighbourhood, Michael spied a small gathering of people. He leaned in to hear what was going on. A minister, standing in the centre of the group, was offering words of comfort. He was urging them to be the best that they could be and to turn away from the violence and crime that dominated the area.

Michael was captivated by the minister's gentle words. He felt they were aimed at him. In that moment, Michael decided that he didn't want to live a life of crime any more – he wanted to be proud of himself. He turned on his heel and walked away from his rendezvous with the gang.

Michael joined the minister's church youth group and started to campaign against drugs and street crime. He sought out and linked up with other like-minded people. Then he decided to seek funding to start up his own organization. He worked hard to raise funds from anywhere he could – from businesses, organizations and the government. Eventually he raised enough money to set up an office and hire people to start working with the young people at risk in the townships.

Today, Michael's organization runs a variety of projects that provide children with food and a safe space to play. It runs camps for young people at risk and shows them a positive alternative to the violent way of life offered by the gangs. Michael's organization has set up projects in more than a hundred South African schools, teaching the importance of communication without violence. The organization also funds counsellors for young people already caught up in crime.

Thanks to Michael, thousands of young people are learning that they can take control of their own lives and future, and escape the vicious cycle of gang violence that has dominated their communities for so many years.

South African gangs

During the apartheid era in South Africa (1948–1994), non-white people were forced by the government to live in townships away from city centres. These townships suffered great poverty, unemployment and a lack of investment in education. Frustrated by their situation many young people formed gangs that terrorized their communities. Drug running, stealing and murder became common. Apartheid is now over, but its legacy of poverty and violence in the townships means that gang membership is still a problem in many South African communities.

▲ Some South African teenagers are tempted to join gangs to protect themselves from the violence of their poverty-stricken neighbourhoods. As gang members they can earn money through dealing drugs, stealing and other crimes. For many of young people, gang life can also be a family tradition, with parents and grandparents often members of the same gang.

Christian's Story
El Salvador

Christian was just 10 years old when he joined the Mara Salvatrucha (MS-13) gang. He was living with his grandmother in El Salvador at the time. It would take him eight years and the support of a former gang member in the United States to escape.

When he was 15, Christian's mother, who was living in Los Angeles, sent for him. Christian arrived to find he had a stepfather, two younger brothers and a baby sister. He felt out of place and alone in this strange new country. He hated school and roamed the streets instead. During his wanderings, he came across MS-13 territory in Los Angeles and was amazed to recognize some members from El Salvador there. It wasn't long before he had returned to gang life. One day, a friend of his was shot during

About MS-13

In the early 1980s a civil war erupted in El Salvador killing around 100,000 people. Many Salvadoreans fled to the United States. Most settled in poor areas of Los Angeles. Young Salvadoreans were soon victimized by local gangs. To fight back they created their own gang — Mara Salvatrucha, or MS-13 — which quickly became one of the most violent gangs in the area. Many members were arrested and sent back to El Salvador, but they continued MS-13 membership there. The Los Angeles MS-13 gang also continued to grow, and branches can be found in many parts of the United States and Central and South America.

◀ A member of Mara Salvatrucha (MS-13) flashes his gang sign out of a prison cell in San Salvador, the capital city of El Salvador. MS-13 is believed to be one of the largest gangs in the world, with members in around 30 countries. There are approximately 10,000 members in the United States, with a further 50,000 in El Salvador, Honduras, Guatemala and Mexico.

▶ Leaving a gang, especially one involved in criminal activities, can be extremely difficult. However, there are organizations, often run by ex-gang members, which offer telephone helplines, counselling and other kinds of support to people trying to escape gangs.

a drive-by shooting. Christian was sitting right next to him. After that, he decided he didn't have the stomach for gang life any more and wanted out.

Two days later, Christian was watching a talk show about gangs when he saw a telephone number that would help him. It was the phone number of an organization that helped young people escape from gangs. Christian called them and spoke to Juan, a former gang member. They both knew that leaving MS-13 would not be easy. In some cases people wanting to leave had been badly beaten or killed by the gang. Others had been killed as traitors several years after leaving. Juan encouraged Christian to talk to his family and get their support. He then advised him to spend less time with the gang and to come to the group's drop-in centre which was run by former gang members.

After several months, Christian decided that the gradual phase-out strategy wasn't working. He decided to ask to be 'jumped' out. The beating he received was so vicious, Christian thought he would die, but he curled himself into a little ball and prayed. After it was over, he staggered to the nearest health centre. The centre treated his injuries and telephoned Juan. Juan took him home to recover.

Today, Christian is working on a building project organized by Juan for ex-gang members and attending school part-time so he can get his high school diploma. Juan makes sure Christian gets to work and school safely, without harassment from the gang. He has enrolled Christian in a tattoo-removal programme, so he can leave all traces of the gang behind him.

Justin's Story
United Kingdom

Justin is now 19. He has lived most of his life on the streets of London as both a gang member and as a prostitute. When someone recognized his potential, he decided to change his life for the better.

When Justin was a baby, his mother had a mental breakdown. To cope, she started drinking heavily and then turned to a drug called crack cocaine. She couldn't look after herself properly, let alone Justin and his brothers and sisters. She also owed people money for drugs. Justin remembers people breaking into the house to look for his mother and to try and find money. Sometimes they would beat up his mother and the children. One man sexually abused Justin when he was four.

Justin spent his time living with different family members, and sometimes neighbours gave him food. He hated going home – it wasn't safe and he was very ashamed of his mother and how bad things were. By the time he was 11, Justin was running wild on the streets and had joined a gang. The gang made him feel like part of a family. The gang leaders told him he could make money to buy food by drug running – taking packages of cocaine, heroin, crack and other drugs across London to dealers. They warned him he would be shot if he didn't do it.

▶ Young people who grow up without family support can experience serious emotional problems, poverty and great hardship. Left to roam the streets, they are not only likely to join gangs, but may also end up as prostitutes, selling their bodies for sex in areas like this and putting their lives at risk.

◄ With the right support it is possible for young people to leave their old lives of crime and despair behind them. Some urban areas have drop-in centres, which can provide advice and support. In Justin's case, the drop-in centre helped him go back to school, offered him counselling and found him a mentor who encouraged him to turn his life around.

Justin made a lot of money as a drug runner – enough to buy food and clothes. But he made more by becoming a prostitute – selling sex to older men. Justin now describes his younger self as filled with guilt, pain and fear. He knew his life was going nowhere and heard of a drop-in centre that could help. The centre was very welcoming and practical. It encouraged the young people who attended to learn new skills and ran a drama group with professional actors to inspire them.

Justin became a regular visitor. He threw himself into drama and was spotted by Annabel, a woman who runs an organization for street children. Annabel told Justin his performance was amazing and that she wanted to help him reach his potential. Justin decided to put his faith in her. He has never looked back. Through Annabel's organization he has received counselling, education and a safe place to live.

Justin has now left the streets and gang life forever, and is studying law at college. He says he will always be grateful to Annabel for believing in him and helping him turn his life around.

Caring for street children

There are organizations all around the world that try to care for street children. Many of them are charities that depend on donations from the public to carry out their work. Some of these organizations fund residential centres where street children can be looked after. Others provide education programmes and medical services, drop-in centres, night shelters and places where the children can get food.

Glossary

apartheid A political system that operated in South Africa from 1948 until 1994. Under this system, non-white people were forced to live separately from white people.

bail A sum of money that someone – often a friend or relative – will pay to a court so that an arrested person can go free until his or her trial.

bisexual Sexually attracted to both men and women.

blog A personal online diary.

Bloods gang A Los Angeles street gang, rivals of another gang, the Crips, and identified by the colour red.

civil war A war between organized groups within the same country.

counselling Help with personal or psychological problems, given by a professional.

Crips gang A Los Angeles street gang founded in the early 1970s. It is now one of the biggest in the United States with approximately 35,000 members. Its members use the colour blue as their identifying symbol.

cyber-bullying Bullying carried out through information or communication technologies such as email, MSN and mobile phones.

drive-by shooting Firing at someone from a moving vehicle.

drop-in centre A place that people can visit without an appointment to get advice or information, or to meet others.

drug running The transportation of illegal drugs.

dyslexia A learning difficulty in which a person struggles to recognize and understand written language, leading to spelling and writing problems.

eating disorder An emotional disorder that can result in someone eating too little or too much food.

geek A term often used as an insult to describe someone very focused on their studies, particularly computers or other technology.

mental breakdown A sudden and serious mental illness that leaves a person unable to cope with the responsibilities of everyday life.

mixed race A term used to describe someone whose parents are from different races.

Pachuchos A gang of young Mexican-Americans formed in the 1930s and 1940s. They wore distinctive clothing and spoke their own dialect of Mexican Spanish, called Caló or Pachuco.

prostitute Someone who offers sex for money.

relocation A move from one area to another.

sex trade The buying and selling of sex.

sexuality The direction of someone's sexual desire – whether they are attracted to men, women or both.

slum A run-down area in a town or city, in which people live in poor housing and unsanitary conditions.

suicide The act of killing oneself.

trial A process that takes place in a court of law, over the course of which a person is found guilty or innocent of a particular crime.

UNICEF (United Nations Children's Fund) An international organization that works to improve the health and education of children in developing countries.

Further Information

Books
FICTION
The Battle of Jericho by Sharon M Draper (Simon Pulse, 2004)
The Bully by Paul Langan (Townsend Press, 2002)
The Outsiders by S E Hinton (Penguin, 2006)
Touching Spirit Bear by Ben Mikaelsen (Harper Collins, 2002)

NON-FICTION
Bullies, Big Mouths and So-Called Friends by Jenny Alexander (Hodder Children's Books, 2006)
I Wrote on All Four Walls: Teens Speak Out on Violence by Fran Fearnley (Annick Press, 2004)
Letters to a Bullied Girl: Messages of Hope and Healing by Olivia Gardner and Emily and Sarah Buder (Harper Paperbacks, 2008)
Stick Up for Yourself: Every Kid's Guide to Personal Power and Self-Esteem by Gershen Kaufman, Lev Raphael and Pamela Espeland (Read How You Want, 2009)

Websites
www.childline.org.uk
Advice and help for young people on wide range of issues, including bullying and gang membership.

www.cybermentors.org.uk
Advice and online help about cyber-bullying.

www.gangstyle.com
An in-depth US site for anyone with experience of gangs. Lots of true stories and support.

www.need2know.co.uk
Advice on life and relationships.

www.redcross.ca/article.asp?id=24700&tid=108
Canadian Red Cross youth site. Full of interesting statistics, practical help and inspiring stories.

Index